SLEEP TIGHT

W9-CNB-649

SLEEP TIGHT

By

B. G. HENNESSY

Pictures by

ANTHONY CARNABUCI

VIKING

VIKING
Published by the Penguin Group
Viking Penguin, a division of Penguin Books USA Inc.,
375 Hudson Street, New York, New York 10014, U.S.A.
Penguin Books Ltd, 27 Wrights Lane, London W8 5TZ, England
Penguin Books Australia Ltd, Ringwood, Victoria, Australia
Penguin Books Canada Ltd, 10 Alcorn Avenue, Toronto, Ontario, Canada M4V 3B2
Penguin Books (N.Z.) Ltd, 182–190 Wairau Road, Auckland 10, New Zealand

Penguin Books Ltd, Registered Offices: Harmondsworth, Middlesex, England

First published in 1992 by Viking Penguin, a division of Penguin Books USA Inc.

10 9 8 7 6 5 4 3 2 1

Text copyright © B. G. Hennessy, 1992
Illustrations copyright © Anthony Carnabuci, 1992
All rights reserved

Library of Congress Cataloging-in-Publication Data
Hennessy, B. G. (Barbara G.)
Sleep tight / by B. G. Hennessy ; illustrated by Anthony Carnabuci.   p.   cm.
Summary: As they are tucked into bed and everything around them is ready
for sleep, two children see what a special place their house becomes.

I S B N 0 - 6 7 0 - 8 3 5 6 7 - 6

[1. Bedtime—Fiction.   2. Sleep—Fiction.]   I. Carnabuci, Anthony, ill.   II. Title.
PZ7.H3914S1 1992   [E]—dc20   91-36464   CIP   AC

Printed in Hong Kong
Set in 22 point Plantin Light.

Without limiting the rights under copyright reserved above, no part of this
publication may be reproduced, stored in or introduced into a retrieval system,
or transmitted, in any form or by any means (electronic, mechanical,
photocopying, recording or otherwise), without the prior written permission
of both the copyright owner and the above publisher of this book.

For Brett Michael
—B.G.H.

To Patricia,
my love and inspiration
—A.C.

Night time

Quiet time

Read our favorite book time

Cozy time

Whisper time

Time to go to sleep time

Who is sleeping?

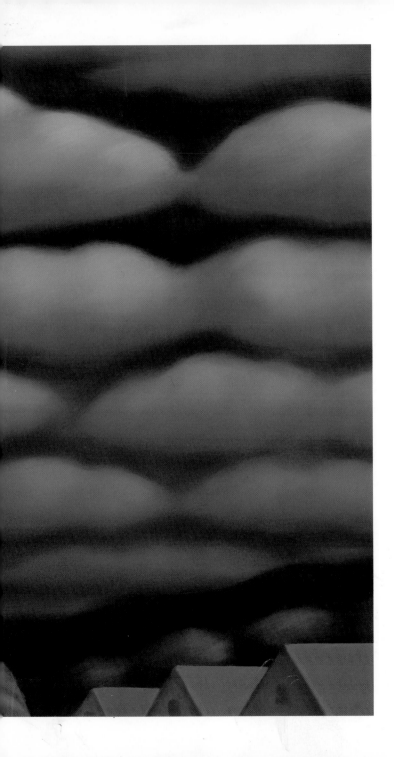

Birds are sleeping in the trees

Clouds are sleeping on a breeze

Trains are sleeping on the tracks

Bugs are sleeping in the cracks

Stores are sleeping in the town

Grass is sleeping on the ground

Birds, clouds, trains, trees

Bugs, cracks, stores, breeze

Grass, town, tracks, ground

Things are sleeping all around

Who is sleeping in our room?

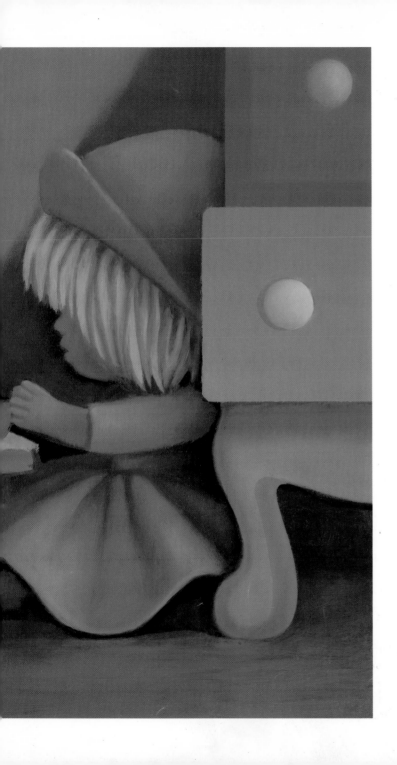

Our socks are sleeping in a drawer

Our shoes are sleeping on the floor

Our soap is sleeping in the tub

Our blocks are sleeping on the rug

Our books are sleeping on a chair

Rabbit's sleeping next to bear

Shoes, chair, soap, blocks

Books, bear, tub, socks

Pillow, blanket, bed, night-light

A song, a yawn, then sleep tight.